# Ellison the Elephant

by Eric Drachman

illustrated by James Muscarello

Kidwick
books

For my parents, who have always encouraged me in everything... even in making funny sounds.   — E.D.

www.kidwick.com

Voices on CD (alphabetically):
Benjamin Drachman (Ellison), Eli Drachman (himself), Eric Drachman (Narrator, Weasel),
Julia Drachman (Eleanor), Rebecca Drachman (Edna), Paula Lozano-Drachman (Mom)

Ellison's original jazz music was composed and produced by Giovanna Imbesi
at TuttoMedia in Venice, CA.  (www.tuttomedia.com)
Bryon "BTrain" Holley (musical voice of Ellison & animal voice accompaniment)
Eric Drachman (animal voice accompaniment)

Scherzo by Gregor Piatigorsky courtesy of The Piatigorsky Foundation
Evan Drachman, cello; Richard Dowling, piano

Text design and layout by Andrew Leman. Set in Kidegorey.

Illustrations were rendered with watercolor, pastel, and colored pencil on
hot pressed watercolor paper.

Printed in Korea
Distributed by National Book Network
Published in Los Angeles, CA  U.S.A. by Kidwick Books LLC

## DISCLAIMER
What follows is a work of the imagination. All the characters and events in this book are fictitious.
No resemblance to real persons, places or institutions is intended or should be inferred.

Publisher's Cataloging-in-Publication
(Provided by Cassidy Cataloguing Services, Inc.)

Drachman, Eric.

Ellison the elephant / by Eric Drachman ; illustrated by James
Muscarello. -- Los Angeles, CA : Kidwick Books, 2004.

p. ; cm. + 1 sound disc.

Ages: 3-7.
CD contains the story, accompanied by sound effects and
original jazz music.
Summary: Unable to make the normal trumpet blast, little
Ellison gets teased by the other elephants.  With encouragement
from his mom - and provocation from his imaginary friend, Weasel
- Ellison finds his very own voice.  The music from his "jazz trunk"
charms and entertains all within earshot.
ISBN 10: 0-9703809-1-7
ISBN 13: 978-0-9703809-1-3

1. Elephants—Juvenile fiction. 2. Self-esteem—Juvenile fiction.
3. Jazz—Juvenile fiction. 4. Imaginary companions—Juvenile fiction.
5. Imaginary playmates. 6. Children's audiobooks. I. Muscarello,
James. II. Title

PZ7.D733 E45 2004                          2004091959
[E]--dc22                                   0410

Ellison was an elephant – a little elephant – and young.
He was a young and little elephant, but not a baby elephant.
His friends and his sister, Edna, could all make their trumpet
blasts like other elephants...

...but not Ellison.

He tried and he tried, but all he got was a little toot.

"See?" cried Ellison. "I don't even sound like an elephant!"

"Ellison, I love your sound," his mother insisted. "It sounds like you!"

"Well, I don't want to sound like me," Ellison answered. "I want to make a trumpet sound like everyone else!"

Ellison's mom got very close and touched him gently with the tip of her trunk.

"Ellison, you are not an ordinary elephant. No sir, you are extraordinary. Even your name is unusual. All the greatest elephants in history were unusual – that's what made them great!"

"But they tease me, Mom..."

"Oh now, Ellison... one day they'll all want to be like you.  In the meantime – you're an elephant – you need to have a thick skin!"

With this, she gave him a motherly squeeze.

Together, they walked down to the watering hole, trunk in trunk, where all the other elephants were bathing.

Ellison liked it when Mom washed his back, but when she sprayed under his chin, the ticklish Ellison giggled and squirmed.

He watched as the others played their noisy games. They squealed and blasted, honked and blared.

Not wanting to be called "Smellison" or "Tootie" again, Ellison made his way up the bank and behind a small clump of trees where he could be alone with his imagination.

There, he tried and tried to make that wonderful, grand call that came so easily to everyone else.  He filled his cheeks with breath and he threw his big ears forward...

...but all he got was a little toot.

Full of despair, Ellison stomped and stormed until he stumbled right over a bush.

# THAT — DID IT!

He kicked that little bush and pulled it from
the ground and shook it with his trunk.

And that was when that bush – YELLED – at Ellison.

"What do you think you're doing?!?
Leave me alone, you – you ELEPHANT!"

"This is unusual," thought Ellison.
"I've been yelled at by all kinds of
animals, but never by a bush.
I'm sorry, little bush," Ellison
apologized. "Are you okay?"

Then, out of this bush – DROPPED – that pesky weasel.

"Don't let it happen again, Smellison!"
he yelled, and he waddled away.

Ellison followed him around the corner, over the hill,
and into a valley, talking as he went...

"Hey – wait up, Weasel – you can't talk to me like that!"

"I'm bigger than you... and I apologized...
and I didn't know you were in there in the first place...
and you can't make me feel any worse anyway, because I can't even
make a trumpet sound like an elephant!  All I can make is a stupid little toot!"

Weasel stopped in his tracks and turned around to look up at Ellison.

"Okay. Do it."

"Do what?" Ellison asked.

"Your sound," Weasel answered. "Stop whining about it and let's hear it!"

"Fine," Ellison agreed, and he blew a sad little sound.

Weasel shook his head. "Yep, that's terrible!
I'd be mad, too," and he disappeared into a hole
in the ground.

Ellison was not afraid of that little weasel. He walked right up, stuck his trunk down the hole, and blew one very crisp clear sound...

...that echoed underground.

What followed was a long silence during which Ellison *was* a little afraid. He wondered if he should have just let Weasel be this time. But then, Weasel popped out of the hole with dirt on his fur and a smile all over his face.

"Now *that* I like," he said, shaking the dirt off. "Do it again!"

"You're making fun of me," replied Ellison.

"No I'm not," Weasel insisted.
"What else can you do?"

"I don't know," admitted Ellison.

"Can you hold it longer?"

Ellison tried...                    ...and he could!

"And can you change the pitch?"

And he did.

"And can you make a
lot of quick notes?

Like *yat*

    *tat*

      *tat*

        *tat*

          *tat?*"

And he did.

"Wow!" yelped Weasel. "This is great!"

"Okay. Okay. Now, close your eyes and look inside.
When you find your voice, let it out..."

Ellison had no idea what a
voice should look like, but he
closed his eyes and looked inside...
and looked... and looked... until...

# ...he found it!

It looked like nothing he'd seen before,
but he knew it right away.
It was his very own voice!

Ellison's legs felt stronger
and his heart grew bigger.

He took in a deep breath and started
with a looooong note that went on. . . . . and on. . . . . and on. . . . . .

...until all of the ears on all of the elephants
in the watering hole turned to listen.
They set out at once, in search of that most
extraordinary sound.

"That's right, Ellison!" hollered Weasel, jumping up and down. "Don't stop now – you've got IT!"

And Ellison did not stop. He made every sound that came from inside and it formed a tune that made him dance.

When the other elephants spied him from atop the hill, they saw and heard what they'd never before seen or heard.

They stood and they watched with their mouths hanging open and before they knew it, all of their trunks were swinging in time to the rhythm of Ellison's jazzy music.

When he came to the end of his brand new tune, Ellison opened his eyes
– and saw – and heard – the whole herd.  They rushed downhill to see
the elephant who invented music.  Leading the pack was Ellison's mom,
beaming from one big ear to the other.

"How'd you do it, Ellison?"

"I had help, Mom –

from Weasel."

"Weasel?" asked Mom. "Your imaginary friend?"

"Yeah — he helped me find my voice and it's
reeeaaaalllly unusual!"

Edna, Eleanor, and Eli crowded in next to Ellison,
begging, "Teach us! Teach us, pleeease!"
Everyone wanted to be as unusual as Ellison.

All of the elephants and some of the other animals, too, danced and sang and kept rhythm while Ellison played his jazz trunk. When the sun went down, the lightning bugs lit up the darkness.

All night long, animals came from everywhere to hear the unusual elephant with the extraordinary sound.